KATIE DAVIS

I'm telling you, Dex, Kindergarten Rocks!

SCHOLASTIC INC.

New York Toronto London Auckland Sydney Mexico City New Delhi Hong Kong

I am Dexter Dugan and I know everything about kindergarten. This is because I am actually going to *be* a kindergartner. Very soon.

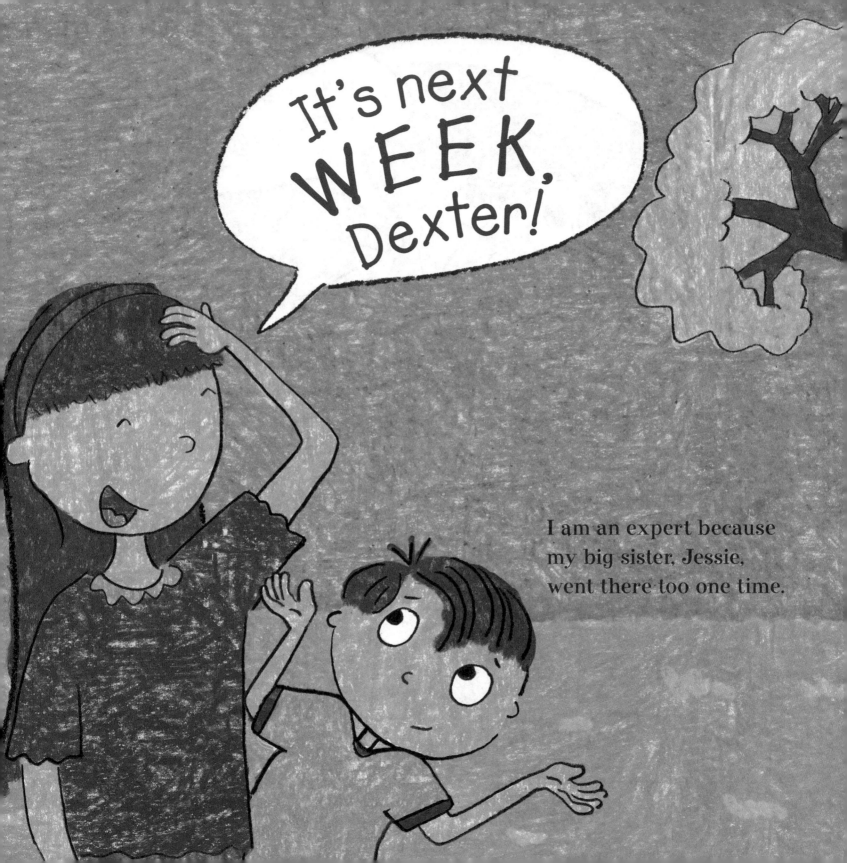

My dog Rufus is an eensy teensy beensy bit scared about kindergarten.

Jessie went to kindergarten a long, long, long, long, long, long, long, long, long, long, long time ago (but she still remembers it even though she's going into third grade).

When Jes went to kindergarten, she wasn't big like she is now.

She wrote like me. And she drew like me, too.

Only not as good.

I got Jessie to help me make a list of things Rufus was scared about.

I'm not worried though.

Kindergarten will be
a piece of cake.

Nooooo problem.

I can't wait.

When the bus came the next morning,
the driver seemed like he knew what he was doing, so I got on.

Rufus was still worried, but Jessie had a great idea.

When we finally got to school, I couldn't wait to see my classroom.

There are some *kind of* good surprises about kindergarten.

For one thing, my friend Joey from preschool was there.
Rufus was so happy to see him, he forgot to worry.

We made art,

and cooked food,

and smushed Play-Doh.

I got to write letters,

and build a gigantic tower,

and play in the
imagination station,

and look at books.

Then we went to the library. That's where you go if you want to know about snails or soccer or outer space or shark guts. You can borrow a whole book all about it and keep it practically forever.

At lunch you get to eat with all your friends in the cafeteria.
It's exactly almost like a restaurant.

And there are people called custodians who clean the whole entire school
and they help you even when you spill your milk by accident
and you are scared you'll get in trouble.

After lunch, everyone goes to recess. Joey says you can't get lost playing
I-Am-A-Monster-And-You-Are-A-Powerful-Monster-Getter
because if someone's always chasing you, how can you get lost?

Rufus was so happy to see me. He knew I'd find him the whole time.

I'm going to learn lots of stuff in kindergarten,
but the thing I learned today was . . .

To my former teachers Mrs. Cook, Mr. Saunders, and Mrs. Ciricillo;
to the fabulous teachers at my kids' school;
to all teachers who inspire and ignite our children every day
—K. D.

Special thanks to:
My children, Benny and Ruby, who let me use their artwork in the book.
Another to Ruby, who, based on her own kindergarten experience, came up with the title.
And Ms. Sugarman, for being an enthusiastic listener, guide, and model, and who is as sweet as her name.

ISBN 978-0-545-34124-0

Copyright © 2005 by Katie Davis.
All rights reserved. Published by Scholastic Inc., 557 Broadway, New York, NY 10012,
by arrangement with Houghton Mifflin Harcourt Publishing Company.
SCHOLASTIC and associated logos are trademarks and/or registered
trademarks of Scholastic Inc.

12 11 10 9 8 7 6 5 4 3 2 1   11 12 13 14 15 16/0

Printed in the U.S.A.   08

First Scholastic printing, March 2011

The display type was set in Lemonade Bold.
The text type was set in Elroy.
Designed by Linda Lockowitz